Billy the Squid

by

Colin Dowland

Colin Dowland was born in Dorset. He studied at
the Royal College of Music and became a school
teacher in 1988. He lives in North London.

Illustrated by Peter Firmin

To Mum and Dad,
Two pearls of wisdom
With love to Annie,
And nonsense-fishdom

Barrington Stoke has enchanted and inspired generations with his stories. He would go from village to village, arriving at twilight and carrying a lantern to light his way and signal his arrival. In the village meeting place he set down his lantern and placed five stones in a circle. Barrington Stoke stood at the front of the circle in the light of his lantern. In the flickering light the children sat entranced while he told the tale. And then another. And then another, until they were tired and ready for sleep. But Barrington Stoke's imagination was never exhausted - he moved on to the next day, the next village, the next story.

First published in Great Britain by Barrington Stoke Ltd
10 Belford Terrace, Edinburgh, EH4 3DQ
Copyright © 1998 Colin Dowland
Illustrations © 1998 Peter Firmin
The moral right of the author has been asserted in accordance
with the Copyright, Designs and Patents Act 1988
ISBN 1-902260-04-X
Printed by Polestar AUP Aberdeen Limited
Printed 1998 (three times) and 1999 (twice)

Contents

Chapter One

Driftwood was a pretty little town under the sea in the mid-west, just off the shores of Thousand Island. It had a bank, a jail, a church, a saloon bar and a general store. An untidy trail of old wooden houses spread along the sand and up into the rocks and reefs beyond.

The fish of Driftwood were simple soles. Shrimps were shrimps and folk knew their plaice. Except for the odd harmless water fight at the Blue Lagoon Saloon Bar, nothing much happened in sleepy, watery Driftwood Town.

That was until today. Right now. A stranger had stormed into town and was making waves at Driftwood Bank.

'Okay, fishface, stick your fins up and back off real slow,' bellowed the gruff voice of a huge and terrifying lobster.

His claws were razor sharp and his face was half hidden by a neckerchief. A black hat with a broad brim half-covered his right eye. Over his other eye was a long, deep scar. He threw four large saddlebags onto the counter and grabbed the goldfish bank clerk by his braces.

'Fill 'em up with gold or I'll fill you full o' rocks,' he ordered, spitting a bubble into the sand and releasing the braces with a twang.

The bank clerk nodded and moved backwards towards the safe without taking his eyes off the scary-looking crook. His glasses were misting up and his fins were shaking uncontrollably.
The lobster snapped his claws together impatiently.

'Get a move on. I ain't got all tide,' he shouted.

The bank clerk tried to keep calm. His shaky fins slowly turned the combination lock back and forth until the safe clicked open. He reached inside and began to fill the saddlebags. When they were full and bulging with all the town's gold, he put them on the counter and backed away.

'You look mighty green around the gills, partner,' chuckled the crook. He wiped a trail of sea-slime from his pink, crusty nose. 'Keep your fins above your head and don't do anything stupid.'

The lobster gave a loud 'Yee-ha'. He then turned and with a flick of his fan-like tail swam off out of the bank, and out of sleepy, watery Driftwood.

Chapter Two

Way out west of Driftwood, near a shipwreck on the other side of Thousand Island, a lonesome bounty hunter sat astride his trusty sea-horse. His hat was pushed back on his head and along all eight sleeves of his well-worn jacket, tassels rippled with the movement of the waves. He pulled a piece of seaweed from his jacket pocket, put it in his mouth and began to chew.

This was Billy the Squid.

Quick, smart and cooler than an iceberg's icebox, Billy the Squid was a sea drifter who rode with the tides. He knew the ocean like the

back of his tentacles. He had travelled through most of it and had seen things that would make your scales stand on end. He was on his way to someplace from somewhere east of no-place. Wherever something fishy was going on, that was where Billy was heading. He would ride into town as a nobody and leave as a hero.

Billy gulped loudly and nodded his head. Something fishy was going on nearby. He could taste it in the water.

Cautiously, he circled the shipwreck, checking for signs of anything unusual. Suddenly his sea-horse stopped in its tracks, tossing its head from side to side. Billy listened. His squid's ink-stinct was right.

'Help, somebody, help!' came a muffled cry from somewhere inside the shipwreck. 'Help us!'

Billy's tentacles twitched and he slowly climbed down from his sea-horse.

Billy knew that he had to be careful. He had foolishly swum into a trap in his younger days when out fishing off the reef with a cousin.

A pair of very strong mussels and a young lobster had ambushed them in the shallows of Thousand Island Bay. He had only escaped by the skin of his suckers. His cousin, a fearless octopus, had lost four legs in the attack. Now Billy did not take any chances. He was not ready for a watery grave just yet.

Slowly, Billy inched through a porthole in the side of the wrecked ship and drifted, listening silently. Once he was sure it was safe, he carefully tip-tentacled through the wreckage in the direction of the shouting.

Billy crept through the gloomy gangways, brushing away rotten seaweed that dangled in front of his face, until he came to a door. The shouting was coming from behind it. He could hear the cries of little ones too.

With one swift tentacle, Billy grabbed the door handle, flung it open and fired. The room was filled with clouds of black ink and the shouting turned to coughing and spluttering.

As the room began to clear Billy could see maps and charts pinned to the walls. A telescope dangled above his head and a globe rested on a large, wooden table. It was the long-forgotten remains of a captain's cabin.

For a moment, Billy could not see where the coughing was coming from. Once the ink had completely cleared, he was amazed to see four oysters, two large and two small, underneath the captain's table. Their shells were gaping widely open and they were tightly tied, back to back, with some of the old ship's rope.

'Thank cod!' gasped one of the large oysters as she saw Billy standing there.

'Can you untie us mister, please?' said the other.

Billy inspected the knots. They were too much for even his nimble tentacles.

'Sit tight, you all,' said Billy. 'I've got an idea.'

Billy put two tentacles to his lips and blew a long, bubbly whistle. After a few seconds, a sleek, muscular-looking fish with a long, jagged nose appeared at the porthole.

'This sawfish will soon cut you free,' reassured Billy.

And sure enough, after a couple of saws from the sawfish, the two oyster children were soon sitting inside their tearful mother's shell.

'We're all mighty grateful to you, mister,' said the father oyster to Billy as the final rope

was cut. 'It was dark and the whole family was asleep. Our shells were shut as tight as could be ...'

'And then this monster came along,' shuddered the mother. 'We couldn't see much. It had huge claws and was far too strong for us. Our shells were forced open in two shakes of a clam's tail.'

'It took all our pearls,' continued the father, his shell quivering with rage. 'Every single one. We're left with nothing. Our shells will take tides and tides to repair.'

The father oyster tried to comfort his wife and the children began to cry very salty tears.

'We'll turn into sea-urchins,' blubbed the youngest oyster. 'Begging on the streets.'

Billy the Squid took off his hat and knelt down by the youngest oyster, patting her warmly on the shell. 'Don't worry kid. I'll get you your pearls back.'

As Billy spoke, he noticed, by one of his many elbows, a few pieces of crusty, pink shell lying beside the young oyster. He picked up a piece, examined it and put it into the inside pocket of his jacket.

'We can't thank you enough, mister,' continued the father. 'Who is it we have to thank?'

'Just call me Billy,' said Billy. 'Billy the Squid.'

The mother oyster gasped. 'Not *the* Billy the Squid who tamed the wild sea-horses at the Rockpool Rodeo ... ?'

But it was too late. Billy was already mounting one of those very same, tamed sea-horses. He didn't like fishing for compliments. He had a pearl thief to catch.

Chapter Three

Meanwhile, back in Driftwood, the sheriff was busy in his office. The sheriff of Driftwood did not just have a sheriff's star pinned to his chest. A star *was* his chest, his body, his head and his arms. Yep, the sheriff was a starfish with a record of arrests as long as all five arms.

'So this crook took off with all the town's gold?' asked the sheriff, who was questioning the bank clerk about the gold robbery. 'And you say he was huge and pink ... ?'

'And crusty, with a scar over one eye,' completed the bank clerk, who was a rather nervous type of goldfish. 'It was terrifying.'

The goldfish put his head in his fins and began to sob quietly to himself. He had found it hard to get used to the salty conditions in Driftwood. He wished he could go back to his old job at the River Bank in Freshwater City on Thousand Island.

'If a goldfish can't look after the gold, who can?' he snivelled, removing his glasses to wipe his eyes.

'Sheriff, sheriff! We've been robbed,' interrupted a halibut with a black eye as he rushed into the sheriff's office. A hobbling haddock with his tail in a sling followed closely behind.

'We were robbed last night, up on Reef Ridge,' the halibut continued. 'We lost some sea-horses. Stolen from outta the barn.'

'We tried to stop him, sheriff,' said the haddock. 'Us and some of the other fish. But he was too quick for us. He turned real nasty and lashed out. One of the cod got badly battered and some shrimps got a real pasting.'

The haddock removed his hat and wiped a tear from his bulging eye.

'I'm afraid the cod had his chips. He was buried this morning at low tide.'

The stunned sheriff held up two of his arms to calm the over-excited haddock.

'You mean,' said the sheriff, thoughtfully stroking his droopy moustache. 'Driftwood has a sea-horse thief?'

'That's right sheriff,' nodded the haddock. 'As clear as tide follows tide.'

'I never thought I'd see the tide when Driftwood would sink so low,' sighed the sheriff, sadly shaking his head. 'First the bank robbery and now stolen sea-horses. Whatever is this town coming to?'

The sheriff stood at the doors of his office and looked down his beloved street. In tides

23

gone by, the most serious crime had been just a missing mermaid's purse. Driftwood used to be such a peaceful town. The jail behind his office was hardly ever used. The lock had rusted solid.

'Tell me boys,' he continued, getting back down to the serious business of catching crooks. 'What exactly did this sea-horse thief look like?'

'He was pink and crusty, with claws as big as a shark's breakfast,' said the halibut holding out his fins to show how big the claws were.

'With a horrible scar above his left eye,' added the haddock.

'That's him,' interrupted the bank clerk, who had been sitting quietly blowing bubbles to himself. 'That's the one who robbed the bank. He was huge and terrifying, with a scar.'

The sheriff nodded slowly.

'Guess you fellas were lucky to come out alive,' he said. 'There's only one person in the whole of the ocean who fits your description. One of the most dangerous crooks that ever swam in the sea. None other than Quickclaw McClaw, the fastest, toughest, ugliest lobster in the west.'

'So, what are we gonna do, sheriff?' cried the goldfish, who proceeded to blow his nose squeakily into a dainty red finkerchief.

The sheriff grabbed his hat, his holster and his water pistol.

'Round me up some of the strongest fish you can find. We leave from the Blue Lagoon Saloon at the turn of the tide.'

Chapter Four

Meanwhile, Billy was hurrying across the bay on his trusty sea-horse. He had a hunch that someone who had a bag full of pearls would be looking for safer waters and shelter on the other side of Thousand Island.

Billy had put away the cunning pickpocket Fingers O-Cod and rounded up the violent Smash 'n' Crab Gang. He had even put the wicked Crayfish Twins behind bars. The oyster family hold-up, however, was as nasty a crime as he had seen in a long tide.

Billy had only travelled a few sea-miles when he came across a couple of large fish from the sheriff's gang sticking up a poster on the side of a reef.

Billy squidded to a halt and tipped his hat at the two fish.

'Trouble, boys?' he asked.

'You could say that, mister,' said the haddock with his tail in a sling. 'Back in Driftwood. The bank's been robbed and someone's been stealing sea-horses.'

'Folks ain't safe in their sea-beds no more,' continued the halibut who was nailing up the poster. 'The sheriff has set up round the rock patrols everywhere. There's a mighty fine reward on this ugly lobster's head. He's wanted - boiled or alive.'

Billy stared at the face on the 'Wanted' poster in front of him and spat out his seaweed into the sand.

'Well, I'll be fried in breadcrumbs!' he exclaimed.

The black, beady eyes of Quickclaw McClaw stared back at him out of the poster. This was no ordinary crook. Compared to Quickclaw, the Crayfish Twins were just small fry.

Quickclaw McClaw was the big fish, the codfather of crime, who terrorised the deep and polluted the sea with his dreadful deeds.

'Which way is it to Driftwood, fellas?' asked Billy.

'Downstream,' replied the haddock, pointing a fin in the right direction. 'Follow the current for a couple of tides. It's just beyond Reef Ridge.'

Billy nodded his thanks, kicked his many heels and rode off at full speed, leaving a cloud of sand behind him.

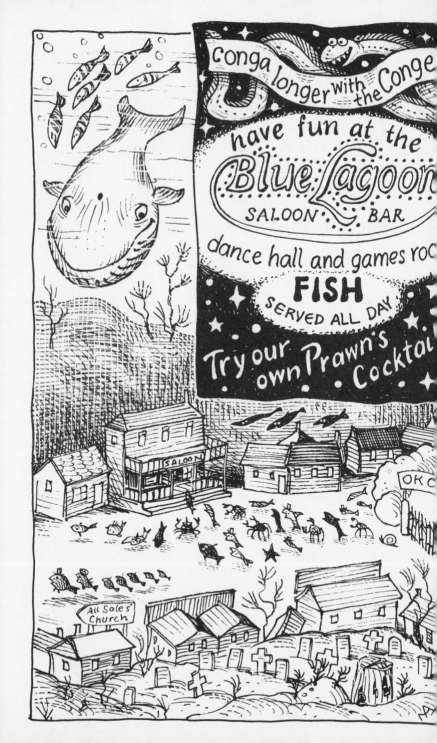

Chapter Five

The Blue Lagoon Saloon Bar in Driftwood was where all the fish went to enjoy themselves. It was a big barn of a place with water-colour paintings of Jellyfish James and Buffalo Brill hanging on the walls. A human skeleton hung over the bar and some fishing nets with large holes in them dangled from the ceiling.

The old seadogs of Driftwood were sitting at tables discussing the bank robbery. A few card-sharks were playing poker at a table and a waitress glided from table to table collecting empty glasses. In the far corner, notes rang out

from a piano. It was too out of tune to play and so a piano-tuna was busy working on it.

The doors of the Blue Lagoon Saloon swung open. The piano went silent and all the fish froze. Everyone stared. All you could hear was the sound of spurred, crusty claws walking slowly to the bar.

'Ye ... ye ... yes, mister?' asked the barman, a small prawn, known for his tasty, pink cocktails.

'My mouth feels like a dried-up river bed, bartender,' growled none other than Quickclaw McClaw, thumping the bar with a heavy claw. 'Give me a bottle of old fisheye.'

The bartender slid the bottle across the bar and scurried away.

Billy the Squid was sitting quietly in a corner, sipping one of the prawn's cocktails and shuffling two decks of cards with four of his tentacles. He had slipped into town unnoticed and was waiting for something to

happen. He knew that sooner or later the mad, bad lobster would turn up, scaring all the fish in the town and showing off his claws.

Quickclaw took a long swig from his bottle and let out an enormous belch. He sure looked like a lobster, but he drank like a fish.

Wiping his mouth with a huge claw, the lobster staggered towards the waitress, who glided backwards to avoid him. Quickclaw was too quick for her and grabbed one of her fins, spinning her round to face him.

'What's the hurry, angel-fish?' he spluttered, taking another swig from his bottle. 'Ain't you ever seen a handsome lobster like me before?'

The waitress tried to pull away, but the lobster tightened his pincer grip, making her drop the glasses that she had collected.

'You've the prettiest fins this side of Finland, missy. Wouldn't you like a pretty little necklace to go with them?'

As he spoke, Quickclaw brought out a beautiful pearl necklace from inside his shell and held it up in front of her face.

'How about it, angel?' he smirked, dribbling from both sides of his crusty mouth.

Billy's tentacles twitched. He called across the saloon bar to the lobster.

'I don't think the lady takes kindly to your manners, mister,' Billy said, politely tipping his hat towards the waitress.

Quickclaw pushed the waitress away and approached Billy's table. He leaned down slowly, put his claws on the table and spoke into Billy's face.

'Reckon you'd better keep your trap shut, little squid,' growled Quickclaw, blasting Billy with his disgustingly fishy breath. 'Now shift your suckers. I wanna sit down.'

'There ain't no room at this table,' drawled
Billy. 'You'll have to find somewhere else to sit.'

'Whaaaat?' bellowed Quickclaw, flashing his
claws in front of Billy's face.

Billy did not move and returned Quickclaw's
cross-eyed, beady stare.

'You'll have to find somewhere else to sit,' he repeated, staring back all the more.

Quickclaw straightened up and bubbles started to seethe from his nose.

'Listen, shrimp. Do you know who you're talking to?' he snapped, slamming his bottle down on the table in front of Billy.

'Yup,' said Billy very calmly. 'I know just who you are. *Thermidor* McClaw,' he grinned. He had done his homework and knew that Quickclaw's real name was Thermidor.

There were some muffled laughs from another table and more laughs from a table next to that. A fat mackerel standing at the bar would have wet himself laughing if he had not been wet already. Soon the whole of the Blue Lagoon Saloon was filled with waves of laughter. Thermidor really was a *very* silly name.

'What did you call me?' growled
Quickclaw.

The saloon bar went silent, but Billy
repeated himself very slowly. 'Therm-i-dor
McClaw.'

The lobster grew pinker and pinker and
looked about to explode.

41

'Only my mother, cod rest her sole, called me that,' he shouted. 'No one calls me that now. Not no one. Never. Do you hear?'

'Oh go boil your head, Thermidor McClaw. I ain't scared of you,' replied Billy without looking up from his game of cards.

'Okay, mister. You've asked for it. We need to settle this once and for all. The OK Coral at High Tide. Be there.'

And with that Quickclaw McClaw grabbed his bottle and staggered out of the Blue Lagoon Saloon leaving the doors swinging behind him.

Chapter Six

It was high tide in Driftwood and the current was as strong as a limpet's grip. Waves of fear were spreading through the town. All around, shutters were closed. Flatfish hid their heads in the sand and the sardines were packed into the rocks, as tight as . . . . . well, sardines.

All was quiet. Only a few tufts of seaweed rolled past the gates of the OK Coral.

Up at the church, the monkfish said a few prayers. All over town jellyfish trembled. A dogfish barked.

The sea-horses that usually packed the OK Coral had been led away at low tide. Now it was just a deserted stretch of shifting sand that was waiting for the big showdown.

Quickclaw McClaw tipped his hat forward to shade his eyes from the sun and sharpened his claws on a rock that he kept inside his shell. Then, pushing open the heavy OK Coral gate, he strode forward snapping his claws nervously. His needle-sharp spurs jangled menacingly at every stride.

Billy the Squid was already waiting for him at the far end of the coral. All eight of his tentacles were ready for action. Quickclaw had taken the bait - hook, line and sinker.

Billy met the gaze of Quickclaw's black, beady eyes and slowly began to walk towards him. When he was close enough to smell the lobster's disgusting breath, Billy stopped.

For a moment, nobody moved.

'Okay squid,' shouted Quickclaw, his voice echoing around the deserted coral. ' . . . . . Draw!'

Billy's tentacles twitched. Then, as quick as lightning, Quickclaw drew his claw and lashed out. Billy was ready and fired. The OK Coral was filled with a cloud of black ink and neither Billy nor Quickclaw could be seen. Then, a flick of a tentacle, the slash of a claw, a flash of pink. Suckers, legs and shell flew in all directions in a tangled, twisted whirlpool of sand and ink.

And then everything went still.

Slowly the water began to clear and after a long, long minute the squid's ink had dissolved into the surrounding water.

There, standing proudly back, polishing one of his eight knuckles on his chest was Billy the Squid. Struggling next to him, all tied up in knots of seaweed with his huge claws strapped tightly shut, was Quickclaw McClaw.

'You ain't got nothing on me, I ain't done nothing,' pleaded the lobster, desperately trying to squirm free.

Billy grinned and held up the pearl necklace in one of his other tentacles.

'I know a family of oysters who would be overjoyed to have these pearls returned.'

Billy held up yet another tentacle holding the piece of pink, crusty shell that he had found next to the oysters.

'And I reckon this piece of shell belongs to you,' he continued, waving it in front of the lobster's ugly face. 'You stole the pearls from them and this is the watertight, waterproof evidence.'

One by one the fish from the town crept out from their hiding places and stood lining the main street. As Billy frog-marched Quickclaw down through the crowd towards the jail, fish began to cheer and wave. They shook Billy warmly by a tentacle or two and then lifted him up over their heads, carrying him the rest of the way down the street.

Billy the Squid had saved Driftwood from the crusty old crook. Quickclaw McClaw was heading for jail, where the mad, bad lobster would get a good grilling from the sheriff.

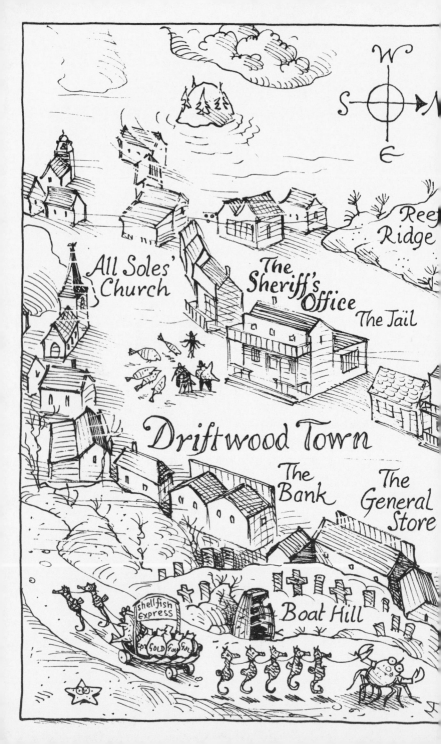

Chapter Seven

At the sheriff's office, the lobster was proving to be a tough shell to crack. In the end, the sheriff had to hold Quickclaw McClaw's head above the water until he turned bright blue.

Then, unable to hold his breath any longer and gasping for water, the lobster finally owned up to all his crimes. Not only did he confess to the pearl robbery, but also to the bank hold-up and the stolen sea-horses. He would go to jail for the rest of his natural sea-life.

The stolen sea-horses were returned to their owners and the town's gold was locked up safely back in the bank. The pearls were returned to

the grateful oyster family, who celebrated with a wild barnacle dance for all the fish of Driftwood.

Music could be heard as far away as the distant shores of Thousand Island. The conger eel led the conga dance and the dolphins gave free rides to all the little fish. Sardines unpacked themselves in their hundreds and the anemones made friends with their enemies. Even the hermit crab came out of his shell for a little jig. Everyone had a whale of a time, including a whale who had swum over to see what all the fuss was about. The celebrations carried on deep into the sea.

For Billy, the capture of Quickclaw McClaw was his finest catch. He was glad that the fish of Driftwood could swim happily about their business once more.

But Billy had another reason to be proud.

You see, Billy never forgot a face. Not one as ugly as Quickclaw McClaw's. They had met many tides ago, when Billy was just a little squid and Quickclaw only a young

nipper-snapper. That was the time when Billy had been fishing off the reef with his octopus cousin. They were set upon by that same young lobster, Quickclaw, and two strong mussels. Billy escaped unharmed, but his cousin had not been so lucky and now had four wooden legs to remind him of that terrible day. He would visit his cousin sometide soon and tell him all about the shoot-out at the OK Coral with Quickclaw McClaw.

The fish of Driftwood had made Billy feel very welcome. They gave him the reward for Quickclaw's capture and threw a big party in his honour. They even asked him to become Mayor of Driftwood.

Billy had been tempted to stay on in the town. It could get real lonesome with only a sea-horse to keep you company at night. He looked at the families of fish that were dancing and singing around the rocks.

Perhaps one of these tides he would settle down, get married and have some little squids of his own. But Billy hated staying in one place for too long. He was happier just drifting with the ebb and flow of the ocean.

Billy always felt like a fish out of water at parties. Squids couldn't dance very well with all those tentacles getting in the way. The waitress from the Blue Lagoon Saloon had asked him to dance and he had trodden on her tail at every step. So, as the rest of the town danced until dawn, Billy crept away to find his trusty sea-horse. He put the reward for Quickclaw's capture in his saddle-bags, and rode silently off in search of his next adventure.

Billy the Squid had other fish to fry.

Other titles published by Barrington Stoke:-

Kick Back by Vivian French   1-902260-02-3

The Gingerbread House by Adèle Geras   1-902260-03-1

Virtual Friend by Mary Hoffman   1-902260-00-7

Wartman by Michael Morpurgo   1-902260-05-8

Screw Loose by Alison Prince   1-902260-01-5

For further information please contact Barrington Stoke at:-
10 Belford Terrace, Edinburgh EH4 3DQ